Written by David Bedford
Illustrated by Brenna Vaughan and Henry St. Leger

First published 2013 by Parragon Books, Ltd.
Copyright © 2018 Cottage Door Press, LLC
5005 Newport Drive, Rolling Meadows, Illinois 60008
All Rights Reserved

ISBN 978-1-68052-541-0

Parragon Books is an imprint of Cottage Door Press, LLC.
Parragon Books® and the Parragon® logo are
registered trademarks of Cottage Door Press, LLC.

I love my Grandpa

PaRragon.

One warm and sunny afternoon, Little Bear went for a walk by the river with Grandpa Bear.

"Should we go for a swim, Little Bear?"

Little Bear shook his head.
"I don't like water, Grandpa," he said.
"Let's just put one paw in," said Grandpa, "and see what it feels like."

Grandpa Bear put one
paw in the water.
"Ah!" he said.
"That feels good!"

Little Bear put only the tip of his paw in. Then he giggled. "The water tickles!" he said, and he put the rest of his paw in and waved it around.

"Wheeee!"

Grandpa Bear put
two paws in.

So did Little Bear.

Then Little Bear put all four of his little paws into the cool water.

"Good job, Little Bear!" said Grandpa.

"You're wading! Now, are you ready to make a splash?"

Little Bear kicked his feet,
making splashes with a

swoosh-swoosh-swoosh!

swoosh-swoosh-swoosh!

Then suddenly ...

Splash!

In jumped Grandpa Bear,
showering Little Bear!

"Yippee!" cried Little Bear.

"Should we go for a swim now, Little Bear?"
said Grandpa.

Little Bear shook his head.
"I can't swim, Grandpa!" he said.

"Let's just float," said Grandpa,
"and see what it feels like. I will hold you."

When Little Bear felt his grandpa holding him,
he lifted up one paw at a time, until …

"You're floating!"
said Grandpa Bear.
"Now, how about some more splashing?"

Little Bear kicked his feet, making more

swoosh-swooshes!

And suddenly ...

"You're swimming,
Little Bear!" said Grandpa.

"Swim, Little Bear, swim!"

Little Bear swam around
and around his grandpa.

"You're the best little swimmer there is," said Grandpa Bear proudly.

When it was time to get
out, Grandpa Bear helped
Little Bear climb out of
the water.

Then they both wriggled and jiggled
to get dry, spraying water all around.
"We're making a rainbow!" giggled Little Bear.

Grandpa Bear gave Little Bear
a warming hug.
"Do you like water now, Little
Bear?" he said, smiling.

Little Bear grinned. "I love water!"
he shouted happily. "And ..."

"I love my grandpa!"